Prop and Prep
on the trail

Marion Kemp and Sheila Lane

Illustrated by Colin Mier

Series editor **Penni Cotton**
Senior Lecturer, Reading and Language Studies
Kingston Polytechnic

To Parents

By sharing books together at home you can play a vital part in helping your child learn to read.

The books at Level 3 in this series are for children who are progressing towards reading fluently on their own. The play format gives the support necessary for children to enjoy reading with you and yet lets them read their own part and thus gain confidence as independent readers.

How to read this book together

▷ Make reading together a comfortable and special time.

▷ **The role of Prop is for you to read and your child reads Prep**. Explain that you don't read out the speaker's name each time – it is just there to help tell you when it's your turn.

▷ Introduce the story slowly by looking at page 5 and talking about the characters. Perhaps your child is already familiar with them from other books in the *Parent and Child Programme*.

Help your child, particularly on the first reading, by giving the difficult words so you don't slow up the pace of the story or by reading both parts initially.

Encourage your child to use the pictures to guess or predict what is happening.

If your child is stuck just give the word yourself. This is far more helpful than sounding out individual letters.

Always praise good guesses – much of the skill in reading is in guessing or predicting what the word will be.

Your child will probably enjoy reading the story with you again and again – this is valuable in building confidence and practising reading.

Always end reading together on a positive note.

Prop Prep, tell Wuff to come out. I've brought him a really delicious breakfast!

Prep Come on, Wuff! Come out!

Prop Oh dear, he's not here!
He's broken his lead and gone!

Prep Where can he be?

Prop He's probably hiding. Let's
call him.

Prep + Prop Wuff! Wuff!

Prop Oh no! I hope he hasn't gone off on one of his adventures!

Prep We must go and look for him. Come on!

Prop But where shall we look? He could be anywhere, let's look for some clues.

Prep Clues! Yes! Let's look for clues.

Prop Come and look through my magnifying glass.

Prep What can you see?

Prop I think – yes! I've found a paw mark.

Prep But is it Wuff's paw mark?

Prop It might be, let's look for another one.

Prep Over here!

Prop Wuff's tracks!

Prep Look, here are some more.

Prop I'm sure they're Wuff's tracks. Come on, Prep! Let's get after that little green rascal. We'll soon have him back.

Prop Can you see something under these bushes?

Prep Yes! I can see something red.

Prop What was Wuff wearing?

Prep His little red coat.

Prop He's hiding from us.
Let's creep up and surprise him.

Prep + Prop Got you!

Prep Look out, Prop! It's not Wuff!

Prop Eeek! It's a horrible red and yellow snake. Quick, let's run!

Prep Yes, come on! Let's look for some more clues.

Prop What's that sticking out round the corner?

Prep A tail!

Prop A green tail with a pom-pom on the end of it.

Prep Wuff's tail!

Prop We've got him this time. Now, both together . . .

+ **Prep**
Prop Got you!

Prep Oh no!
It's NOT Wuff!

Prop It's this lady's umbrella!

Prep Come on, Prop, run!

Prop Phew! I thought she was going to get us with her umbrella.

Prep She was cross!

Prop What shall we do now? Come on, Prep, you're the one with the ideas.

Prep Let's look for another clue.

Prop I'm beginning to think Wuff is lost for ever.

Prep No he's not, look at this.

Prop Prep! That's a link from a dog's lead.

Prep Wuff's lead.

Prop You're right!

Prep Come on, then!

Prop He's come into this toy shop.

Prep **Wuff loves toy shops.**

Prop There he is, in the corner next
to the clockwork monkey.
Can you see him?

Prep **Yes, that's him!**

Prop I think he's fallen asleep.
Let's wake him up.

+ Prep
Prop Wuff! Wuff!

Prep Wake up, Wuff!

Prop Stop! Look at those huge teeth.
It's not Wuff!

Prep Come on! Let's
get away!

Prop Oh dear, we were wrong again, and now it's starting to rain. I give up!

Prep Don't give up!

Prop This rain is making me rusty and my legs are getting stiff.

Prep We've got to find Wuff. Come on!

Prop Wait a minute! There's a garage. Let's get some oil for our joints.

Prep Here's the oil.

Prop Pour it all over me, Prep.
Get it in my joints and in my
grippers. Mmm! That's
much better!

Prep Put some in my ears.

Prep + Prop Lovely! Lovely!

Prep I feel better now, Prop.
Hey, look over there!

Prop Lights! And music!
It must be the fun-fair.

Prep Let's go!

Prop Good idea, Wuff loves music
and bright lights.

Prep And having fun!
Come on! Let's go to
the fair.

Prop I'm sure we'll find him here.

Prep **Oh! Look over there!**

Prop It says: To the ghost train.
Let's see if Wuff's on the train,
shall we?

Prop Isn't this fun?

Prep I . . . I . . . think so.

Prop Ghosts! Skeletons! Giant spiders! Wow! They're going to get us, Prep!

Prep I don't like it in here!

Prop Don't be scared,
Prep, they're not real.

Prep I wish I was
at home.

Prop It's all right, Prep, I can see
daylight. We're nearly out.

Prep I didn't like that!

Prop Hall of mirrors, this looks more fun. Let's find out how we really look, you'll like this.

Prep Do we have to pay?

Prop No. It says:
Walk in, walk in,
free fun for all –
the fat and the thin,
the short and the tall.

Prep Wow! Look at me!

Prop Oh, Prep! You look so funny!

Prep I'm not fat like that.

Prop I'll try this mirror. Ow! I'm as thin as a stick.

Prep That was great!

Prop But I still don't think we'll find Wuff here.

Prep Yes, we will.
We must find him.

Prop But where? There are roundabouts and dippers, that enormous octopus and a big wheel.

Prep Wuff won't be on the big wheel.

Prop No, he'd be much too scared.

Prep But he likes going round and round.

Prop You're right! Let's try the roundabout.

Prep OK, we're in!

Prop Just in time, it's started!

Prep We're going round!

Prop Help, I'm getting dizzy!

Prep Look! Look! I can see something green and red — it's Wuff!

Prop Got you, Wuff! We've come to take you home, you little green rascal!

Prep Prop! Look over there!

Prop Quick! Get in with Wuff! That man looks angry.

Prep Press that big black button. Go on, press it!

Prop	We're taking off!
Prep	Up and away!
Prop	Hurray! We'll soon be home.
Prep	Home with Wuff!
Prop	What an adventure! What trouble will you get into next, Wuff?